Meet the *Young* and *Famous* in Sports:

Mike Tyson
Chris Mullin
Debi Thomas
Roger Clemens
David Robinson
Vinny Testaverde
Rony Seikaly
Boris Becker
Spud Webb
Kristie Phillips
David Rivers

And more!

Take a good look at the up-and-coming in the world of sports. Find out how they broke in, where they came from and what they hope to accomplish. Filled with photographs, this fun-to-read collection of short sports biographies will inspire young athletes everywhere.

Books by Daniel Cohen

GHOSTLY TERRORS
THE GREATEST MONSTERS IN THE WORLD
HORROR IN THE MOVIES
THE MONSTERS OF STAR TREK
MONSTERS YOU NEVER HEARD OF
REAL GHOSTS
THE RESTLESS DEAD
SCIENCE FICTION'S GREATEST MONSTERS
STRANGE AND AMAZING FACTS ABOUT STAR TREK
SUPERMONSTERS
THE WORLD'S MOST FAMOUS GHOSTS

Books by Daniel and Susan Cohen

HEROES OF THE CHALLENGER
THE KID'S GUIDE TO HOME COMPUTERS
ROCK VIDEO SUPERSTARS
ROCK VIDEO SUPERSTARS II
WRESTLING SUPERSTARS
WRESTLING SUPERSTARS II
YOUNG AND FAMOUS: HOLLYWOOD'S NEWEST
  SUPERSTARS
YOUNG AND FAMOUS: SPORTS' NEWEST SUPERSTARS

Available from ARCHWAY Paperbacks

YOUNG AND FAMOUS:
SPORTS' NEWEST SUPERSTARS

DANIEL AND SUSAN COHEN

AN ARCHWAY PAPERBACK
Published by POCKET BOOKS
New York   London   Toronto   Sydney   Tokyo

The sports superstars pictured on the front cover are, clockwise from the top: Debi Thomas, Roger Clemens, Mike Tyson, Kristie Phillips and Boris Becker.

AN ARCHWAY PAPERBACK *Original*

An Archway Paperback published by
POCKET BOOKS, a division of Simon & Schuster Inc.
1230 Avenue of the Americas, New York, NY 10020

ISBN: 0-671-68725-5

First Archway Paperback printing November 1987

10 9 8 7 6 5 4 3

AN ARCHWAY PAPERBACK and colophon are
registered trademarks of Simon & Schuster Inc.

Printed in the U.S.A.

IL 4+

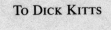

To Dick Kitts

CONTENTS

YOUNG AND FAMOUS:

SPORTS' NEWEST SUPERSTARS

SOME AMAZING PEOPLE

Get ready to meet some amazing people.

You already know that all the people in this book are terrific athletes. And you know that they all became famous while still young. You've probably already seen many of these young sports superstars on television. You may have been amazed by the skill, strength, or grace of their performances. You may have wondered, "How did these people become so good, so young?"

That's what we're going to tell you in this book.

You will find out that what these young athletes have accomplished on the field, in the ring, on the court, or wherever they may have performed is only half the story. The really amazing part is their lives beyond sports.

Take Debi Thomas, for example. Right now she's the best woman figure skater in America and one of the best in the whole world. Being a world-class figure skater is more than a full-time job; the training, the practice, and the traveling are exhausting. Most skaters are worn down by the schedule. Debi does it all, and she's also a premedical student at one of America's top universities. She is doing enough for two people or more.

Boris Becker is another example. He's probably the most famous person in his native Germany, but he doesn't really like it. Oh sure, being rich and famous is fine. But poor Boris couldn't leave his house without being mobbed. Worst of all, the crowds kept him from doing what he wanted to do most of all in the world—play tennis. He had to leave the country.

Mike Tyson, the youngest heavyweight boxing champion in history, thinks back on his own hard and troubled childhood and recalls that many of the kids he knew then are gone now: "Some dead, others in jail. I know how easily I could have joined them." But at the age of thirteen, Mike got a chance to turn his life around completely. He grabbed that chance and held on to it.

Chris Mullin is a Brooklyn "gym rat"—a high compliment, by the way. He started playing basketball when he was practically a baby, and he made himself a great player by simply working harder and longer hours than anyone else. And he loved it.

Rony Seikaly grew up in war-torn Lebanon,

where they don't play much basketball. He moved to Greece, where they play a little but not much. When he got to college, he had to start competing with guys who had been playing basketball all their lives.

In July 1985, Roger Clemens sat on the Boston Red Sox bench in tears. His arm hurt so badly that he was afraid he would never pitch again. In August 1986, Notre Dame basketball star David Rivers lay in the tall weeds beside a rural Indiana road, bleeding heavily after a terrible auto accident. Both of these athletes triumphed over their injuries. They not only survived, but they came back stronger than ever.

Here are the personal stories of some of today's hottest young sports superstars.

1

MIKE TYSON

A TV interviewer once asked Mike Tyson if he had been a delinquent when he was younger.

"Yes," Tyson replied quietly, "but I was a sweet delinquent."

Mike wasn't kidding. This twenty-one-year-old boxing powerhouse from the mean streets of Brooklyn is probably the most famous young sports superstar today. He's also one of the most complicated and most interesting.

In November 1986, Mike knocked out Trevor Burbick in the second round to become heavyweight boxing champion of the world at the age of twenty years, four months, and twenty days. That made him the youngest heavyweight champion ever.

There are a number of different boxing groups and associations. Each one claims the right to name its own heavyweight champion. In the Burbick fight, Mike became WBC heavyweight champ. A few months later, in March 1987, Mike won an easy decision over James "Bonecrusher" Smith to become WBA champ. There are one or two other fighters who claim to be heavyweight champion of the world, but no one takes them seriously anymore. Mike Tyson is truly the undisputed heavyweight champion of the world—the first one in many years.

As for anyone else who might claim the heavyweight title, "Let 'em come," Mike says. He's more than willing to fight them all.

Everything about five-foot-eleven-inch, two-hundred-seventy-pound Mike Tyson radiates strength, power, and determination. He doesn't wear a fancy robe with his name embroidered on the back. He doesn't wear any robe at all. If it's cool, he wears a towel, poncho-style, with a hole hacked out for his head.

There are no fancy trunks for Mike either. He always wears black. In a championship fight, the champ always has the right to select the color of his trunks. The opponent cannot use the same color trunks, or he is fined five thousand dollars. Just to irritate Mike, Burbick—the champ at the time—chose black trunks. Mike paid the fine and wore black anyway. Since he is now champ, he doesn't have to worry about paying fines anymore.

Mike Tyson. *(Focus on Sports)*

Mike doesn't wear socks either. He says that this simple way of dressing makes him feel more like a gladiator, an ancient Roman fighter.

When Mike steps into the ring, he is absolutely determined to win. His opponent knows that, too, and most find his determination and strength intimidating.

Mike's life, like his boxing outfit, is extremely simple. Some boxers have become known for their lavish life-styles, their parties, their fancy clothes and fancy cars. Though Mike is now a millionaire, his life-style is anything but lavish. He fights often and is in training almost all the time. That means early to bed so he can be up doing roadwork early in the morning. Out of the ring as well as in, Mike dresses simply. His main hobby, which he carried over from his boyhood in Brooklyn, is a remarkably gentle one—raising pigeons.

An interviewer once asked Mike if he had many dates. Mike said that with his fight and training schedule he really didn't have time for dates. But then he thought for a moment and added, "I'd make time for Lisa Bonet."

Right now Mike Tyson is at the very top of the boxing world. His future prospects look almost unlimited. A lot of boxing experts say he will be as good as Muhammad Ali, Rocky Marciano, and Joe Louis. You can't get better than that. Mike also has that extra something, that star quality.

Even people who don't care about boxing are attracted to Mike Tyson.

When Mike was growing up, he didn't have much of a future to look forward to. He was born in the tough Bedford Stuyvesant section of Brooklyn. He never knew his father and was raised by his mother, Lorna. His mother hated violence of any kind. Mike has an older brother, but when he was young his closest friend was his sister.

Mike was a shy and gentle boy. It's not easy to be shy and gentle in a place like Bedford Stuyvesant, and he was often picked on. Life got even worse for him when the family moved to the tougher Brownsville section of Brooklyn. Mike was about ten at the time, and he became a target for all the neighborhood bullies. They would steal his money and his clothes and beat him up. Although Mike's basic nature may have been shy and gentle, he was growing up physically. At ten, he was already bigger and stronger than most of the boys his age.

One day someone pushed Mike too far. An older boy tried to steal one of his beloved pigeons. Mike struck back ferociously and beat the boy up. Suddenly all the rage he had been holding in was released. It was a moment that changed his life.

Mike gained new respect from the boys in the neighborhood, and he gained a new set of friends. They were older and tougher, and they were streetwise. They not only fought, they robbed and mugged. At age eleven, Mike was picked up for taking part in an armed robbery. The older boys held the guns, and Mike "just put everything in a bag."

Mike makes no excuses for the turn his life took. Though he was only eleven, he knew what he was doing. No one led him astray; he just wanted to be accepted as part of the gang. He also knew his future was limited and felt that he was going to wind up either in jail or dead. It wasn't that he didn't care; he just didn't see any other way to live or any other way to be accepted. If he didn't pick on others, they would pick on him.

His mother tried to stop him, but it didn't do any good. The once shy and gentle boy became "obnoxious." He wouldn't listen to his mother, and he would barely talk to her.

Mike stopped going to school. He was always being arrested by the police for different crimes. He was in and out of detention facilities. Finally the courts decided that Mike Tyson was simply out of control. He was sent to the Tryon School for Boys in upstate New York. Called a "training school," Tryon is in actuality more like a prison for young offenders. Tryon was a long way from Brooklyn, and Mike knew the next step would be adult prison. He didn't see any way to get off that road. Mike Tyson was now all of thirteen years old.

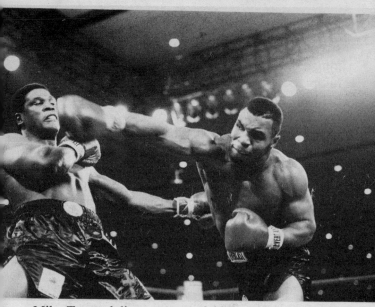

Mike Tyson delivers a powerful blow to Trevor Burbick in the fight that made him the youngest heavyweight champion ever. *(Wide World Photo)*

The Tryon School was filled with tough kids. Mike quickly became one of the toughest. He was so mean that he was put in what was known as the "Bad Cottage"—a place where only the worst of the worst were sent. After a fight with another boy, it took two attendants to get control of Mike.

Mike Tyson practically didn't know how to read, and he was so sullen and withdrawn that people at the school suspected he might be mentally retarded. At that moment in his life, almost everyone, including Mike himself, predicted that his future would be violent, bleak, and short.

Then Mike got a second chance, and, most importantly, he was able to take advantage of that chance.

Mike was spotted by a former boxer named Bobby Stewart, who worked with some of the boys at the Tryon School. The first time Stewart saw Mike, he was handcuffed and being led by two guards because he had just been in a fight. Stewart was impressed by the size and power of the five-foot-eight-inch, two-hundred-ten-pound thirteen-year-old. He described him as being "built like a tugboat."

Mike heard that Stewart had been a pretty good amateur boxer, and he desperately wanted to learn to box. Stewart knew that there is lots more to boxing than just raw power. What a good boxer needs most of all is discipline. He wasn't sure that this violent and sullen boy would ever have the discipline to be anything but a street fighter.

Stewart offered Mike a deal. If Mike would start really working in his classes, then Stewart would teach him to box. Stewart wasn't sure Mike could do anything in school. He just wanted to make sure Mike was trying. Mike accepted the deal, and he did try. He started paying attention in class for the first time in years. In a couple of months, Mike's reading level shot up from third grade to seventh grade. All his teachers were amazed.

They hadn't thought it was possible. The difference was that Mike now felt he had a reason to learn and a reason to pay attention.

As fast as he was learning in the classroom, Mike was learning even faster in the ring. He would spar with Stewart, and soon the experienced boxer could barely keep up with him. The thirteen-year-old kid was hammering him in the ring. Stewart realized that Mike Tyson was no ordinary boxing talent. He had the potential for greatness. Mike started needing more training than Stewart could offer alone, so Stewart called up an old friend named Cus D'Amato.

D'Amato was a boxing legend. Not only was he a great teacher and trainer of boxers, but he was something even rarer—an honest fight manager who really cared about the welfare of his fighters.

It's no secret that the sport of boxing has a very shady history. Managers have often cheated their fighters. Fighters who had made huge amounts of money during their careers frequently wound up broke and in debt. Managers and promoters took all their money. Most fighters were tough kids like Mike Tyson who didn't know anything about the sorts of contracts they signed. They also didn't know how to handle the money they made. The fight business in effect was really controlled by gangsters.

The business of prize fighting still has lots of problems, although it's a lot more honest now than it was twenty or thirty years ago. A fighter has a better chance of keeping the money he earns. A lot of the change is because of Cus D'Amato. He helped to break the gangster stranglehold on boxing. It wasn't easy, and it wasn't safe. For many years D'Amato feared for his life. His home was guarded by huge, fierce dogs. He had to be very careful about going out.

One of D'Amato's fighters, Floyd Patterson, was the youngest heavyweight champion in the world until Tyson came along. When Patterson quit boxing, he still had his health and enough money to last the rest of his life. Another D'Amato fighter was José Torres, the light heavyweight champion of the world, who is now the commissioner of boxing for New York State. Torres also earned enough money to be able to quit boxing before he was seriously hurt. Boxing is a tough sport, and too many professional boxers have to keep at it for too many years because they need the money. The key to success is to be able to quit while you're still healthy.

Cus D'Amato lived in the town of Catskill, New York, and ran a small fight school there. Young fighters would come from all over the country to train with this master teacher. So D'Amato knew what he was looking for in a young fighter. The first time he saw thirteen-year-old Mike Tyson in the ring, he thought he saw star material.

D'Amato made a startling prediction. He told

Mike that if he wanted to live at Catskill and really learn what he was taught, then he could become the youngest heavyweight champion in the world.

Mike recalls thinking D'Amato was "a crazy old white dude." But it was what he wanted to hear. D'Amato took legal custody of Mike, and the boy moved from the Tryon School to the big country house where the legendary trainer lived.

Over the next six years, the old trainer and the kid from the streets of Brooklyn became more like father and son than trainer and fighter. Under D'Amato's guidance, Mike Tyson's basic gentle nature began to emerge from behind the wall of rage he had built up. In the ring, Mike is as tough as he was in the days when it took two guards to hold him down. Out of the ring, he's thoughtful, soft-spoken, and considerate.

Everything about Mike changed. Once he became famous, reporters lined up to interview him. He was a popular guest on TV talk shows. Perhaps you've seen him. It's hard to believe that when Mike first moved to D'Amato's Catskill place he barely talked at all.

There were certain techniques that Cus D'Amato taught all his fighters. One was the so-called peekaboo style in which the fighter holds both hands in front of his face. Floyd Patterson used that style a lot. Mike has modified the style. But D'Amato always believed that the real secret to boxing success is in the mind. The will to win is more important than skill. He repeated his philosophy about the need for discipline and character over and over again to Mike, until now it has become part of Mike's own philosophy. People who knew D'Amato say that sometimes Mike sounds just like him.

Will and skill are fine, but there are lots of determined and skillful young fighters in the world. In order to be a real success, a fighter also needs to have his career managed very carefully. A boxing career only lasts a few years. A fighter can't afford too many mistakes. When starting out, a fighter needs the right fights. He can't fight anybody too experienced and get beaten early in his career. He may be seriously hurt and then get the reputation of being a loser. On the other hand, he can't fight just anybody at all. If he has the reputation of fighting only "bums," boxing people will begin to regard him as a "bum." He also has to be noticed by the boxing writers and promoters. A lot of what makes a successful boxing career goes on in business offices, not in the gym.

Cus D'Amato died at the age of seventy-seven on November 4, 1985. It was a tremendous psychological blow to Mike. He was already known as a promising fighter, but his career hadn't really taken off. Mike wishes that D'Amato had lived long enough to see another one of his fighters crowned champion. Mike is even sadder about his mother, who died of cancer in 1982. He realizes that while she lived his mother knew him only as a kid running wild in the streets. "I never got a chance to talk to her or know her," Mike admits.

D'Amato had died at a critical moment in Mike's career. He had only had twenty-six amateur fights, and he had just turned professional. After D'Amato's death, Mike's promising career was put into the hands of comanagers Jim Jacobs and Bill Clayton. Jim and Bill, both shrewd boxing professionals, had worked with D'Amato for years. They picked all of Mike's opponents carefully, and they made sure the right people got to see him fight. They got stories in the press and on television about how Mike had a difficult time finding sparring partners because he hit so hard. Within ten months and only a dozen fights, Mike Tyson had become a boxing star. Practically everyone was predicting that he would be the future heavyweight champion of the world.

Of course, none of the shrewd promotion would have worked without Mike. He did his part by winning all of his fights, most by early-round knockouts. Mike was also exciting to watch. Since the great days of Muhammad Ali back in the early 1970s, most heavyweight fighters, even the best of them, were dull, dull, dull. Mike Tyson, on the other hand, was anything but dull.

Jacobs has what he believes to be the world's largest collection of fight films and tapes. Mike became a student of boxing history by watching the great fighters of the past in action. Mike spends a lot of his time watching and analyzing fights of many years ago. He feels that one day he can be right up there with the greatest, but not quite yet.

People have been calling Mike great for so long now that he's embarrassed by it. "I'm not great yet," he says. "I'm still just a kid."

Mike's March 1987 championship fight with "Bonecrusher" Smith is an example of what he is talking about. Everyone figured that Mike would win by an early knockout. But he didn't, and, worse, the fight was just plain boring. As soon as Smith, a big puncher, realized that he couldn't hurt Mike, that he could barely hit him, he decided that the only thing he could do was survive. He kept grabbing Mike so he couldn't punch. That went on for twelve rounds. Mike won an easy decision. He said it was one of the easiest fights of his life. At the end he was barely out of breath. The judges gave him every round. But a more experienced fighter would have known how to keep from getting tied up by an opponent who doesn't really want to fight anymore. Mike and his trainers went back to the gym to make sure that didn't happen again. Mike won his next fight by a knockout.

Fame and fortune are wonderful. Sometimes they can also be hard to take if they come very

One of the many clinches during the Mike Tyson–
James "Bonecrusher" Smith fight. *(Wide World
Photo)*

quickly. Some young athletes haven't been able to handle their sudden success very well. In a few cases, they have even allowed success and money to destroy them. Mike Tyson, who is certainly richer and more famous than he ever dreamed of being back in Brooklyn or even a few short years ago, seems to be handling it all very well.

Jacobs, who along with comanager Clayton handles Mike's finances, is amazed that Mike doesn't really seem to care about money very much. "Whatever the opposite for extravagance is, that's Mike," says Jacobs. "He asks for very little spending money, and he doesn't spend very much."

Fame doesn't scare Mike either: "I prefer to be alone, but it's no problem. I always knew I'd be a media star or something like that."

So Mike Tyson is essentially a loner. He trains, he watches fight films, and he raises pigeons, whom he calls "my brothers and babies."

But Mike Tyson is also lonely. There has been a lot of pain in his life—not the sort of pain you suffer in the ring when you get hit, but the pain of loss. He would like to share his wins with old Cus D'Amato, and he would like to see his mother proud of him. He knows that those things can never happen.

Mike Tyson has come a long way in twenty-one years. And he still has a long way to go. He is the youngest heavyweight champion ever, and he has a good chance of becoming the greatest of all time.

He also knows that boxing can't go on forever: "Right now boxing is the most important thing in my life. But I know in the end it can only be a small part of my life. One-tenth of my life."

As we said, Mike Tyson is a complicated and interesting young man.

To contact Mike Tyson, write:

Mike Tyson
Catskill, New York 12414

2

CHRIS MULLIN

Meet Chris Mullin, gym rat. This particular gym rat is six-foot-six, weighs two-hundred-twenty-two pounds, and plays guard on the Golden State Warriors. Basketball fever first struck Chris when he was a little kid dribbling a ball down the driveway of his family's small house on Troy Avenue in Flatlands, Brooklyn, New York.

The whole Mullin clan is hooked on basketball. When Chris's father, Rod, isn't at his job as a customs inspector at New York City's Kennedy International Airport, he's probably home watching basketball on television along with Chris's mother, Eileen. Rod used to play the game just for fun on the playgrounds of Brooklyn when he was young.

Oldest son Roddy Mullin was captain of his college basketball team when he attended Siena

College in Loudonville, New York. Chris's older brother John kept up the tradition by playing guard at Bridgeport, and his youngest brother, Terence, followed in Chris's footsteps onto the basketball court at Xaverian, a small Catholic high school in lower Manhattan. The daughter of the family, Kathy, a nurse, left basketball to the boys, but the one boy in the family who grabbed the basketball and never slowed down was Chris.

Chris (nicknamed "Mo") Mullin was a winner as far back as fourth grade, when he came in first in a national foul-shooting contest. He began his legendary high school career at Power Memorial. While Chris was at Power, the school won the freshman and JV city championships. But Chris wasn't happy with the Power program, so he switched to Xaverian High School, even though he had to sit out an entire year before he could play.

There could be nothing worse in life for Chris Mullin than sitting out a basketball season. Some kids would have wasted the time, but Chris saw the delay as a challenge. Mullin the Magnificent did not desert the gym. He practiced, then practiced some more. He took up running. He trained hard, whipping his body into top athletic condition, and he was more than ready to face the fans during his first game.

Never in the history of Xaverian had so many fans come out to watch their team. Mullin's name

Chris Mullin in his St. John's days. (*Courtesy St. John's University,* © *Mike Martin*)

was magic. Chris didn't disappoint the crowd. He made seventeen of the team's first twenty-one points, scoring thirty-eight for the game. During his senior year, he averaged twenty-five points and twelve rebounds a game. Xaverian went on to win the New York state championship, and people began to say that the easiest way to win a basketball title was simply to have Chris Mullin on the team.

College was next on Chris's agenda. Duke wanted him. So did Virginia and Notre Dame. There was only one problem with these schools— they weren't in New York. Chris wasn't tempted by the lure of faraway places. Spacious campuses, green with grass and trees, meant nothing to a city kid like Chris. A wide range of extracurricular activities also held no attraction for him. He wanted to stay home with his family and friends. Fortunately for Chris, New York City has a school which boasts a terrific basketball team—St. John's University in the borough of Queens. So Chris went there.

If ever there was a perfect melding of student and school, this was it. Chris loved St. John's, and St. John's loved Chris. When he wasn't eating, sleeping, or studying, he was shooting baskets in the gym. Chris often practiced till the clock struck one A.M. But he was no flashy egotist; he worked hard, but not so he could earn all the glory. He was a team player. St. John's coach Lou Carnesecca praised Chris for his unselfishness on the court: "Some players can make themselves look good. Chris makes everybody look good."

Whether or not Chris Mullin wanted to be singled out as a lone superstar, New York is the media capital of the world. His achievements did not go unnoticed. Even the great Larry Bird of the Boston Celtics heaped praise on the college superstar. By the time he graduated, Chris had proved to be one of the most highly honored college basketball players ever. He was selected to every all-American team as a senior and practically every all-American team as a junior. In 1985, he won the prestigious John Wooden Award, given to the top college basketball player in the country. He was also named Player of the Year by United Press International and the Basketball Writers' Association.

Besides being Big East Conference co–Player of the Year along with Georgetown's Patrick Ewing, Chris Mullin led his team to the NCAA tournament's final four in his senior year and was the tournament's leading scorer. He was named Most Valuable Player of the 1985 West Regional and the ECAC Holiday Festival, and for the fourth year running he was the Most Valuable Player of the Joe Lapchick Memorial Tournament. He finished his college career as the all-time leading scorer in the Big East Conference and at St. John's. Add to these glowing accomplishments that Chris was the all-time leader at St. John's in games played, steals, and free-throw percentage. One of the high points of his amateur basketball days came when he played on the 1984 Olympic gold medal–winning U.S. team.

Chris faced his greatest challenge when he began playing in the National Basketball Association. Just as high school star athletes sometimes see their careers spiral downward in college, so college basketball stars sometimes flop in the NBA. Steady, reliable, practical Chris, creator of great plays, had everything going for him except one thing—he was a hometown boy. Chris Mullin seemed rooted in the concrete sidewalks of his old neighborhood. So when Chris (seventh overall) was selected as first-round draft choice by the Warriors, it meant a major move was in the offing. Chris would have to live in California. Could he cope with the change?

When Chris first got to California, he was homesick. But a gym rat belongs in a gym, and the dedicated, hardworking Chris just went right on doing what he'd always done. He played basketball. Contract negotiations kept him out of training camp and the first six games of the season his rookie year. But the day he signed his contract, he stepped out onto the court, played twenty-four minutes, and scored the winning basket of the game. It was a memorable debut. He finished up the season ranking first on the club

Chris Mullin. *(Courtesy Golden State Warriors)*

and second in the NBA in free-throw percentage, the second highest free-throw percentage for a rookie in NBA history.

Chris had done it. He had shown the world he was meant for the NBA. He had shown himself he could succeed outside New York. He went on to a great season the following year, and, as for California, he decided he liked the state. Chris Mullin, the boy from Brooklyn, was now the golden boy of the Golden State.

Still, when the Warriors came east for a game in the Meadowlands Arena in New Jersey, Chris's family, friends, and fans were out in full force to see their hero. One devoted fan even stole Chris's number 17 jersey from the locker room before the game started. Once again, Chris didn't disappoint his admirers. The masterful Mullin led his team to a win just as he'd done at Xaverian and St. John's. But after all, when it comes to being a winner, Chris Mullin's had plenty of practice.

(There have been persistent rumors that Chris will be traded to the New York Knicks. At the time of this writing, however, no trade has been made.)

To get in touch with Chris Mullin, write:

Golden State Warriors
Oakland Coliseum Arena
Oakland, California 94621-1995

3

DEBI THOMAS

She's the whiz kid of the eighties and the first black world-champion figure skater who is also a champion student. The big question for Debi Thomas is, can she continue doing it all at once? Well, if anybody can, it's super high achiever Debi. When she's not on the ice, she can usually be found reading an organic chemistry or biology textbook.

Debi attends Stanford University in California. It's one of the top schools in the country. What's more, she's a premed student. Premed is tough, and at Stanford it's double tough. But Debi's goal is to become an orthopedic surgeon specializing in sports medicine. So she's majoring in medical microbiology. Quite a challenge!

If becoming a doctor seems an ambitious goal, consider what else Debi hopes to achieve. She'd like to win an Olympic gold medal. If premed at Stanford means hours a day of study, going for the gold means hours a day of skating practice, aerobics, and workouts on the Nautilus machine. Winning the Olympics would put Debi up there with American skating stars Peggy Fleming and Dorothy Hamill. But the skater Debi seems to resemble most is Tenley Albright, who glided her way to fame by winning in the 1956 Olympics and who later became a surgeon.

Partly because she is the first black to rise so high in the world of figure skating and partly because media publicity today is far more intense than in 1956, no skater has ever been under as much pressure as Debi Thomas. The camera's always trained on her, whether she's at the rink or in the classroom. Aware of just how much time her studies would take, Debi did try to give up skating a couple of years ago. After all, even her coach, Alex McGowan, doubted anyone could become a skating champion unless she devoted her entire life to achieving that dream.

But Debi discovered that she missed skating too much to give it up. A true competitor, she also missed the zest of formal competition. She found out that she needed both school and skating to be at her best. Just skating was boring. Just studying gave her nothing to take her mind off her books. So she opted for both. But that meant getting very little sleep while needing lots of energy. Yet some-

Debi Thomas. *(Focus on Sports)*

how Debi even managed to find time for friends and a social life at college despite her fiendish schedule.

But even Debi can't always pull off miracles. Take the 1987 U.S. Figure Skating Championships in Tacoma, Washington. Schoolwork had forced Debi to delay training for the nationals, as the U.S. championships are called. Besides getting a late start preparing for competition, Debi strained a muscle in her leg from weight lifting. During competition, she had no problem with the basic moves called compulsories, and she skated well during the short program.

But then came the long program. Ordinarily, Debi is a very strong skater. Watch her on television, and you'll see the five-foot-six, one-hundred-sixteen-pound skater whip across the ice at breakneck speed and then hurl herself upward in a powerful leap. Before her skates can touch the ice again, she twirls in the air like a dazzling spinning top. Her return to the ice is always firm yet graceful.

But at the 1987 nationals, Debi stumbled on her very first triple top loop in the long program. The rest of her performance lacked its usual sparkle, and the championship title went to Jill Trenary. Losing was a blow, but, because skating isn't her whole life, Debi was able to handle the loss well. Losing certainly didn't destroy her great competitive spirit, and, after all, she had come in second.

She took the silver medal again in the 1987 world championship, overcoming injuries to skate beautifully. However, East Germany's Katarina Witt skated even more beautifully and took the gold. But Debi had already proved herself a superstar by defeating Witt in the 1986 world championship. When Debi Thomas captured the gold, Witt was an established champion, previous winner of both the world figure skating competition and the Olympics.

Nobody makes it to the top alone, and, like any other young athlete, Debi needed someone on her side. Sometimes it's a coach or a teacher who steps forward to help a young athlete. Though Debi has received excellent training and lots of emotional support from her skating coach, the person who's believed in her the most and who's done the most for her is her mother, Janice.

Janice Thomas is a high achiever in her own right. She has a master's degree in business administration, works as a computer programmer, and has a wide range of interests and hobbies. Debi's father also works for a computer company as program manager. Though Debi's parents are now divorced, when Debi was small she lived with her mother, father, and older brother, Richard, in Poughkeepsie, New York. Eventually the family moved to San Mateo County in California.

Janice Thomas is not the kind of woman who lives through her children. But she is a person who respects genuine achievement. She values education highly and believes in giving children the chance to explore new ideas and learn where their talents lie. Debi's brother chose to study mathematics and today he's a graduate student in the math department at UCLA.

Skating is something Debi discovered for herself on her own. When Janice was a child, she lived in Wichita, Kansas. It was the era of segregation, and blacks weren't allowed to use the local skating rink. Janice grew up knowing very little about skating. Things were different for Debi, who became enchanted with the sport at the age of five when she saw her first ice show and went skating at the local mall whenever she liked.

Later Debi would give both ice hockey and basketball a try, but neither gave her the thrill of performing solo on the ice. By the age of nine, Debi started participating in figure skating competitions. Janice encouraged Debi and saw to it that she got the skating lessons she so craved. Janice also spent three hours a day driving her daughter to Redwood City Ice Lodge and back when she was in high school. In between trips, Janice drove herself to work.

Meanwhile Debi had to keep up with her schoolwork and put in a six-hour-a-day practice stint on the ice. Of course, Debi and her mother could have taken the easy way out. Debi actually tried it. The easy way out meant quitting school

Debi Thomas. *(Focus on Sports)*

and relying on tutors instead. Debi went that route when she was in eighth grade. She ended up returning to regular high school, however, because she felt she wasn't learning enough from studying solely with tutors. She needed a thorough education if she was to realize her dream of becoming a doctor.

So Janice drove the endless miles and Debi worked double overtime in her academic subjects and her figure skating. Finding the money to finance Debi's skating career was tough. Skating lessons take money, rinks aren't free, and skates cost plenty. The beautiful costumes skaters wear in competitions are also expensive. Somehow Janice always found a way to come up with the money, though there were times when Debi had to take time off from her training for financial reasons.

In the past, skaters were not allowed to earn money through their skating until they became professionals and went on to skate at ice shows. The best time for a skater to turn professional is after a big Olympic win. Figure skating is a very popular Olympic sport, and a skater who wins a gold medal can often command big money by doing commercials and endorsing products.

Thanks to a change in rules, the U.S. Figure Skating Association now allows amateur athletes to do commercials, as long as the money earned is set aside in a trust fund. Debi's star status has already won her an agent, lots of interest from big corporations, and freedom from the stress of trying to come up with the thousands of dollars a year it takes to finance an amateur skating career.

These days Debi gets tons of fan mail from people who find her life inspiring. In 1986, the California State Assembly held a ceremony to honor her. They honored Debi's mother, too. Score a few points for California. Janice Thomas is also a winner. As for Debi, she's a champion in more ways than one. The future Dr. Thomas is one very special skater who mapped out her own future against the odds and without a single role model. Well, she's a role model herself now for millions of people.

To get in touch with Debi Thomas or to find out more about figure skating, write:

U.S. Figure Skating Association
20 First Street
Colorado Springs, Colorado 80906

4

ROGER CLEMENS

On a summer day in 1985, twenty-two-year-old
Boston Red Sox pitcher William Roger Clemens
found himself in so much pain that he began to
cry. The gifted right-hander with the ninety-seven-
mile-an-hour fastball couldn't even warm up.
Worse yet, Roger didn't know why his arm and
shoulder hurt. He thought about all the promising
athletes whose careers had been cut short by
injuries. Was this to be the end for him?

Up until that moment, if anyone had seemed
headed for greatness it was Roger Clemens. In
1983, Roger had pitched the University of Texas
Longhorns to the College World Series Championship win. After college, he spent a short stint
in the minors, but he began pitching for the Red
Sox as early as May 1984. Roger was busy living
up to his nickname, "Rocket," until he pulled a

muscle in his right forearm in August and had to sit out for the rest of the season. Then, less than a year later, the whole nightmare started all over again.

So what if he loved baseball? So what if he'd worked hard to get where he was? None of that mattered if he couldn't pitch anymore. On that summer day, July 7, 1985, Roger Clemens feared he would go down in sports history as just another promising pitcher whose career never got off the ground. He worried that within a year his name would be forgotten.

Because Roger was a tough competitor, he tried playing hurt, but a visit to the Hughston Clinic in Columbus, Georgia, revealed the need for shoulder surgery. Like it or not, Roger was placed on the disabled list. On August 30, a very frightened Roger had the operation he needed. He had every reason to be scared. Surgery doesn't always turn out to be the answer to a pitcher's problems.

Fortunately, the doctors discovered that all that was wrong with Roger was a fragment of cartilage. Once it was removed, Roger could swivel his arm freely without pain. Still, operations aren't magic cure-alls, and the question remained: Would Roger Clemens be able to pitch like a pro again?

While waiting to find out, he didn't sit around and mope or feel sorry for himself. He fought back. Roger was barely out of the hospital before he began strengthening his arm by lifting weights.

Roger Clemens. *(Courtesy Boston Red Sox, photo by Peter Travers)*

Back home in Texas, he continued doing exercises.

The following baseball season found him one of the hardest-working young players in the major leagues. When he wasn't lifting weights, he was running or studying the techniques and records of hitters. As for how well he could pitch, he showed the world on April 29, 1986, when he sank the Seattle Mariners as few teams have ever been sunk before.

The Red Sox were at home in their tiny jewel of a ballpark. Historic Fenway Park has seen a lot of excitement over the years but little to equal what happened that April night. In nine innings, Roger Clemens struck out twenty batters without giving up a single walk. Instead of going down in the record books as a might-have-been-great sidetracked by a serious injury, the six-foot-four, two-hundred-fifteen-pound pitcher was the king of the mound. And he did it in a park so small that it is referred to as a pitcher's graveyard.

To understand just how great Roger's achievement was, consider the stats. The old record of nineteen strikeouts was first set more than a hundred years ago in 1884 by Charles J. Sweeney of the Providence Grays. Tom Cheney of the Washington Senators once struck out twenty-one batters, but it took him sixteen innings to do it. In 1969, Steve Carlton of the Cardinals struck out nineteen Mets, but Carlton's team still lost the game. Clemens's Red Sox won theirs, beating the Mariners three to one.

Tom Seaver struck out nineteen Padres in 1970, but that was during a National League game which meant Seaver didn't have to face the smashing power of a designated hitter. The one pitcher Roger Clemens admires most in the world is Nolan Ryan, who struck out nineteen batters in 1973. But he walked two. Clemens's triumph of twenty strikeouts and no walks is in a class by itself.

The phenomenon named Roger Clemens was making rapid progress toward the Baseball Hall of Fame in Cooperstown, Ohio. After his twenty-K game of glory, the Hall of Fame asked him to send a game ball, his spikes, and a cap. Cheerfully, Roger sent them off, but other glittering honors would come his way that 1986 season.

For starters, Roger Clemens won the American League MVP award, the Cy Young Award, and the all-star game MVP, the only pitcher ever to win all three in the same season. As if that wasn't spectacular enough, he was selected as the *Sporting News* Player of the Year. The only other pitchers in the history of baseball to earn the Cy Young, the league MVP and the *Sporting News* Player of the Year all in the same season were Sandy Koufax in 1963 and Danny McLain in 1968. Boston sportswriters voted Roger the Boston Red Sox team MVP award, and he closed out the

Roger Clemens. *(Focus on Sports)*

regular season with an amazingly low 2.48 Earned Run Average. Roger was a key reason why the Red Sox played in the World Series, the first World Series they'd qualified for since 1975.

Where does a success story like Roger Clemens's begin? In the minors? In college? In high school? In Roger's case, the challenge of baseball began where it begins for a lot of kids—in the Little League.

By the age of nine, Roger was striking out batters by the dozen in his Little League division in Dayton, Ohio, the small city where he was born. Roger was lucky to have an older brother who was quite an athlete. Randy Clemens would later play baseball and basketball at Mississippi College, and it was Randy who saw to it that Roger played on Little League teams staffed with kids who were older and more experienced than the fourth-grade pitching wonder.

After their father died, the boys moved with their mother to Houston, Texas, where Roger's interest in sports didn't lag. At Spring Woods High School, he won three letters as a football defensive end and two more as a basketball center. But there was nothing like baseball, and before he graduated he was clocked as throwing the ball at over 80 mph. He loved to watch the Astros, and he could generally be found inside the dome when the team played home games. Most of all, Roger kept his eye on the great Nolan Ryan.

Roger Clemens's first brush with the majors came when he was a high school senior. Drafted by the Minnesota Twins, he was sorely tempted to say yes. But deep inside, Roger, who was only seventeen, knew he lacked the maturity to aim for the big time just yet. Though he was worried that he might have blown a chance that would never come again, he accepted a scholarship to San Jacinto Junior College and said goodbye to the Twins.

Giving himself time to grow up turned out to be the right decision for Roger, who won all-American honors at San Jacinto. His second shot at the majors came after he'd completed his junior college studies. The Mets scouted him and decided they liked what they saw. Roger believed he was ready for pro ball now and would have signed with the Mets in a minute, but the Mets ended up deciding otherwise. Even top teams make mistakes.

When the University of Texas offered Roger a scholarship, he took it. Once again, he proved his worth, earning all-American honors and capping off his college baseball career in a dream-come-true win when he beat Alabama 4 to 3 in the final game of the College World Series for the NCAA title. As a sign of things to come, he struck out the last six batters. This time around, nobody could argue that he didn't belong in the major leagues, and the Red Sox snatched him up. In the draft, Roger Clemens was nineteenth overall.

Roger Clemens. *(Courtesy Boston Red Sox)*

His pro debut came in Winter Haven, Florida, where he was so good the Red Sox wasted no time promoting him to double-A. He wowed the fans in New Britain, too, and soon found his way to Fenway. Then came great pitching followed by very scary injuries and finally the 1986 season, which was truly a season in the sun.

When Roger Clemens isn't suited up and at the ballpark, you might find him jogging. Jogging is one of his few hobbies. Board games are another. These he plays at home, which is where you'll find him most of the time. Religion is a central part of Roger's life, and so is family. He enjoys being with his wife, Debbie, and baby Koby. Home for the Clemens family is a Boston apartment during the baseball season and a house in Katy, Texas, the rest of the time.

The 1987 season started out in a stormy way for Roger, thanks to a contract dispute which kept him off the team but didn't stop him from working out on his own. Working hard and setting records is what Roger Clemens is all about.

Though stats as sensational as Roger's might make a lot of pitchers conceited, the young ball player from Texas is a polite and modest person. He even went so far as to describe himself as "a nobody" to an Associated Press reporter. It's hard to imagine Roger Clemens a nobody. But as he sees it, at the start of every new season he's just, "Oh-and-Oh like everybody else. There's no doubt in my mind I can pitch, but I don't care who you are. You have to prove yourself again."

Roger Clemens will keep on proving himself again and again. He knows that Cooperstown is calling!

To get in touch with Roger Clemens, write:

Boston Red Sox
Fenway Park
Boston, Massachusetts 02215

5

DAVID ROBINSON

Once upon a time, there was a kid named David Maurice Robinson who didn't play much basketball. Oh sure, he enjoyed an occasional pickup game, and because he stood well over six feet tall, he joined his high school basketball team when he was a senior. But he didn't work very hard at basketball because he wasn't very interested in it.

He was the brainy sort. He liked to read books and play the piano. Math was his favorite subject, and he preferred computers to basketballs. Because he was tall and good-looking and made friends easily, nobody labeled him a nerd. But nobody labeled him a future sports superstar either.

So he went his quiet way without hype. The media didn't pay any attention to him. Colleges with top-rated basketball teams ignored him. After scoring a whopping high 1320 on his College

Boards, he gained entrance to the U.S. Naval Academy. There David Robinson prepared for his future, a future that didn't seem to include basketball. But just like any story that begins "Once upon a time," this one has a magic ending. At Navy, David grew up and up and up to become a spectacular college basketball superstar. He may even become one of the greatest pro basketball players of all time.

Let's start at the beginning. David Robinson was born in Key West, Florida, to Ambrose and Freda Robinson in 1965. The middle child in the family, he has an older sister, Kim, a graduate of Howard University, and a young brother, Charles. Ambrose was a Navy sonar technician, and growing up in a Navy family encouraged David to set his sights on the Naval Academy at Annapolis, Maryland.

Military families tend to move around a lot. Eventually Ambrose retired, and the Robinsons moved to the Washington, D.C., area, where Ambrose found work with a defense contractor. David started school in Virginia Beach, Virginia. He could already add and substract like a human calculator even before he entered first grade. Once in school, he was placed in a special program for gifted children.

A doer and a thinker, David became deeply interested in literature, carpentry, social studies, and electronics as he advanced through elemen-

David Robinson. *(Courtesy U.S. Naval Academy)*

tary school. By high school, his knack for computers had led him to take advanced computer courses at nearby colleges. He enjoyed tinkering with things and put together a six-foot screen-projection TV set which he built from a kit. That kept him occupied for a few weeks.

He found time to try gymnastics and later boxing. A self-taught musician, his favorite composer is Beethoven, and the day just wouldn't be complete for David if he didn't scrunch his giant form onto a piano stool and strike the right chord. He would strike the right chord in more ways than one in college.

Recruiters were looking elsewhere when David graduated from Osbourne Park High School. But this may have been a blessing in disguise. Many highly recruited young athletes who are touted by the media as superstars-to-be fold under the pressure. Others sometimes turn out to be early bloomers who wilt by their junior year in college. David could take basketball or leave it, so he was free to develop athletically at his own rate in his own way and to pursue other interests, such as the Academy's Black Studies Club.

During his first year at Annapolis, he opted to play basketball but he didn't enjoy it and often thought of quitting. The main reason he stuck with the team was because he was flattered to have made it at all. Nobody considered him anything but a routine player.

Robinson began to emerge as David the Dominator in his sophomore year, putting the Middies on the basketball map by taking them to their first NCAA tournament in twenty-five years. But he really made the world sit up and take notice the following year, when he led the Academy to thirty wins and five losses and brought Navy to the NCAA final eight. Many experts predicted that in 1987 he'd bring them to the final four.

Along the way, David set a lot of personal records, including the highest blocked-shot total for a single college game. He was shipshape in the 1986 world championships, outplaying the seven-foot-two Russian Arvidas Sabonis, a key reason why the United States won the gold. He capped the 1986–87 basketball season by taking the unranked Midshipmen to their third straight Colonial Athletic Association tournament win. Third in the nation in scoring and rebounding, David was the top vote-getter in nominations for the Associated Press Player of the Year in college basketball. Cable network ESPN's popular commentator Dick Vitale also picked David as Player of the Year.

David Robinson's accomplishments seem even more amazing when you consider that the Naval Academy is rigorous and demanding and that, basketball or no basketball, David had to study hard. Tradition plays an important role in the creation of a naval officer, and normally David would be expected to serve five years in the Navy after graduating from the Academy. After all, the Naval Academy is not just another college. It has a special purpose: to train future leaders of the armed forces.

When it comes to making the grade, David gets an A, but the late growth spurt that made him a hoops star presented special problems for the Navy. While at Annapolis, David Robinson grew six inches. Today he stands a looming seven-foot-one and weighs a powerful two hundred and thirty-five pounds. No one is sure if he's stopped growing yet.

On a Navy jet, David would have to fly with his knees pressed up against his chest. His height literally disqualifies him from being a fighter pilot. Aboard a ship, he can't even sleep unless curled up in a ball. Confined spaces are definitely out for tall-as-a-tree David, and since there's nothing but confined space on a ship, he's disqualified from serving on one.

Because he's too big for boats and planes, the Navy has decided that David won't be required to serve five years after all. His commitment has been shortened to two years, although he will have to spend four additional years in limited service. Not one to shirk his duty, David is more than happy with the arrangement.

Because of his commitment to the Navy, you probably won't see David Robinson play pro bas-

David Robinson. *(Courtesy U.S. Naval Academy, photo by Phil Hoffman)*

ketball just yet. But when he does, it will be something to behold. In the meantime, between the Navy, reading, piano, math, electronics, and his girlfriend, Stephannie, who's a student at George Mason University, Ensign Robinson will be busy. But he'll sail right into the NBA ranks one of these days. Get ready to salute his arrival!

————————

To get in touch with David Robinson, write:

Naval Academy Athletic Association
U.S. Naval Academy
Annapolis, Maryland 21402

6

VINNY TESTAVERDE

People magazine writer Ron Arias compared University of Miami quarterback Vinny Testaverde to "Smallville's Clark Kent." Off the field he's shy, excessively polite, and serious. But before he goes out for a game, it's as if he slips into a phone booth somewhere and strips down to his Superman outfit. Because on the field he's just super. As the sportswriters like to say, "He has an arm like a rifle." He's quick and able to scramble to avoid charging linemen. He's also big for a quarterback, six-foot-five, and he's heavy, weighing well over two hundred pounds, and very strong. He can bench press three hundred twenty-five pounds. Most surprisingly of all, he's very aggressive and not afraid to take a hit and to hit back. He's not just a passer; he's a complete player.

Vinny's not the sort of quarterback who likes to

Vinny Testaverde. *(Courtesy University of Miami)*

run out of bounds or fall to the ground to avoid being tackled. He's ready to challenge linebackers who outweigh him by fifty pounds or more. He sounds aggressive: "I'm not scared to take a hit, and I'll go and hit someone myself. It's like a personal battle between me and the other team. I don't want anybody to win a game over me."

With some athletes, that sort of tough macho attitude on the field is reflected in a tough, sometimes arrogant, attitude off the field. Not so with Vinny. When the game is over, it's back to being Clark Kent again. Sportswriters, who interview a lot of athletes, say that Vinny is one of the most modest and even-tempered.

Vinny doesn't mind having the reputation for being a nice guy: "Some athletes get fame, then aren't nice afterward. I don't want to be like that."

The most surprising thing about Vinny is that he's basically a shy person. He once flunked a speech course because he was afraid to stand up in front of the class and talk. He can give speeches now, particularly when accepting awards, but he will never become one of football's famous loudmouths.

At a time when there has been a lot of bad publicity about college athletes, Vinny seems destined to become one of college football's best role models. During his career at Miami, there were never any scandals attached to his name. He doesn't drink or smoke. He doesn't act arrogantly with the fans who crowd around him for autographs, which he gives out freely.

As a class assignment, fourth graders from a Pennsylvania school had to write to their favorite college player in 1986. Most of the players responded, but Vinny, not normally the most talkative of athletes, sent a three-page handwritten letter. The letter was full of advice like "Don't ever be afraid to ask for help. Only dumb people don't ask questions." The fourth graders were so delighted by his reply that they sent him a cassette tape of the whole class singing "Happy Birthday" (he turned twenty-three on November 13, 1986). This time Vinny sent back a *five*-page letter.

In 1986, Vinny Testaverde, as quarterback for the University of Miami Hurricanes, was everybody's pick as the top college football player of the year. He was the easy winner of the prestigious Heisman Trophy awarded to the most outstanding player. So many people picked Testaverde so early in the season that some sportswriters complained that there wasn't any suspense in the Heisman Trophy voting that year.

But Vinny wasn't one of those players whose talent developed and was recognized early. His rise to the top of the college football ranks was steady but slow. He'd always wanted to play football. He started playing in the Pee-Wee League in his hometown of Elmont, Long Island.

His father, construction worker Al Testaverde,

says Vinny practiced all the time when he was a kid, trying to emulate his idols like Joe Namath and Terry Bradshaw. "His love for the game is unreal," says Al. Al himself was a big football fan and spent a lot of his free time throwing the football with his boy. Like a lot of fathers and sons, they both dreamed about making it big in professional football someday.

At Sewanhaka High School, Vinny didn't suddenly vault to the top of the team. In fact, he spent most of his high school career sitting on the bench. It wasn't until his senior year that he got to be the school's starting quarterback, and then he led his team to an 8-and-0 regular season and earned a high school all-American honorable mention. An all-around athlete, Vinny also earned varsity letters in baseball as pitcher and first baseman.

At the University of Miami, Vinny wasn't an instant success either. The problem was that there was another quarterback on the team, a fellow by the name of Bernie Kosar, who led Miami to a national championship and then went on to success in the NFL. For most of his career at Miami, Vinny was backup to Bernie.

Vinny didn't really enjoy being number two: "I never screamed or yelled or complained or anything. I was thinking those things, but I never came out and said it. I just went out and practiced."

It wasn't until he was a junior in 1985, the year Kosar graduated, that Vinny got his first shot as starting quarterback for the Miami Hurricanes. At the start of the season he was a relative unknown. By the end of the season everybody who was interested in college football knew the name Vinny Testaverde. In his first regular season as quarterback, he passed for 3,238 yards and twenty-one touchdowns. He was fifth in the balloting for the Heisman Trophy. In the beginning of the 1986 season, he was practically everyone's pick for all-American quarterback. He didn't disappoint those who had high expectations for him. Vinny led his team to a number one ranking throughout the regular college season.

Vinny had hoped to end his college career with a win over the number two team, Penn State, in the Fiesta Bowl in Arizona. A win would have made Miami national champion once again. But it wasn't to be. The Fiesta Bowl was a game in which everything seemed to go wrong. Miami receivers kept dropping passes, and Vinny himself, normally the most accurate of passers, threw an astounding (for him) eight interceptions. He did some great scrambling on the field, but that wasn't enough, and Penn State won 14 to 10.

Before the Fiesta Bowl, the pressure on Vinny was tremendous. Sportswriter Rick Reilly observed, "Since winning the Heisman Trophy, Testaverde has been Public Target Number One."

Vinny Testaverde poses with the Heisman Trophy that he won for being the outstanding college football player of 1986. *(Wide World Photo)*

Everyone figured that Vinny would be the NFL's number one draft choice. "I don't think there's any question he's the first pick," said one football executive. Said another, "Testaverde sits up there right now so far above the second pick . . . this year it drops off pretty quickly after that first pick." All this meant that when Vinny joined the professional ranks he was going to be able to command a great deal of money. Naturally, a lot of people wanted to represent him. Al Testaverde says that before the Fiesta Bowl about a hundred and fifty people called wanting to be Vinny's agent. That's a lot of added pressure for a young man. Vinny finally signed with top sports agent Bob Woolf.

On November 25, 1986, Vinny was riding his motor scooter, and it crashed. He didn't seem badly hurt, but no one knew for sure because he didn't play another game until the Fiesta Bowl in January 1987. Discussing the accident later, his father remarked, "It was worse than the public knew."

The week before the game, the usually even-tempered and polite Vinny seemed tense and short-tempered. And in the end he played a bad game.

But all athletes, even the greatest, have bad games now and then, and the better you are, the more pressure you are going to have to handle. There are always those who will say when you win that it was because you had easy opponents. When you lose, those same people will say that it proves you weren't as good as you were supposed to be. Vinny has been under lots of pressure before, and he's had his disappointments. He has always snapped back stronger than ever. He has all the skill and strength to become a huge success in professional football. And those who know him best say that he has the character and the determination as well.

As expected, Vinny was picked first in the 1987 NFL draft. He signed a multiyear, multimillion-dollar contract with the Tampa Bay Buccaneers. The lowly Buccaneers hope that Vinny will be the key to rebuilding their entire team.

Vinny Testaverde is going to be a major force in football for years to come.

———————

To get in touch with Vinny Testaverde, write:

Tampa Bay Buccaneers
One Buccaneer Place
Tampa, Florida 33607

7

RONY SEIKALY

They take basketball seriously at Syracuse University in Syracuse, New York, where fans turn out in record numbers to watch the Orangemen play in the vast Carrier Dome. The pride of the Orange is a six-foot-ten center named Rony Seikaly who has a lot of other things besides talent going for him. To start with, he is very good-looking. He is also very wealthy. He used to own a four-wheel-drive Renegade and a BMW at the same time, both gifts from his family. Rony's accomplishments include more than basketball. Rony, who lists his home as Athens, Greece, speaks four languages—Arabic, Italian, English, and Greek. Clearly, Rony Seikaly is no mere jock.

Measuring up as Big Man on Campus is easy for the towering Rony, who has to escape from the spotlight rather than seek it out. To ensure some privacy for himself, he lives in an apartment off campus and has an unlisted phone number. This hasn't stopped dozens of girls from trying almost any ploy to meet him, including phoning Syracuse basketball coach Jim Boeheim and begging to be introduced to Rony. One female student went so far as to call Rony's aunt, claiming she'd found his wallet and wanted to return it.

Given all his advantages, Rony's devotion and discipline as an athlete seem all the more admirable. Though for some students college basketball is a ticket to an education, that's not true for Rony. With or without basketball, college was in his future. So was the option of helping his father, Fred, run the family shipping business. A lot of people in Rony's position would just take life easy. But Rony is a hard worker who has set his sights on the big time—the NBA.

Rony's certainly got the credentials. In his freshman year at Syracuse, he was a starter in every game. He led the team in rebounding, scored in double figures eleven times, was in double rebounding seven times, blocked fifty-nine shots, and made the Carrier Classic all-tournament team. He made the Eastern Basketball all-freshman team, was Big East Rookie of the Week twice, and was selected for the Big East all-rookie team.

He started every game at center his sophomore year, was the team's leading rebounder again, and

Rony Seikaly. *(Courtesy Syracuse University)*

scored an average of ten points per game. Ranked sixth nationally, with three blocked shots per game, Rony set an SU record with ninety-seven blocks for the year. He was second in the Big East in blocks and third in rebounding. He made second team all–Big East. Big East all-tournament, and honorable mention all-American.

This was only the beginning for Rony Seikaly, who kept on soaring. He was one of the big reasons why SU had a dazzling 1986–87 season. Rony's postseason play was even more spectacular. The agile Rony was super, leading SU to the final four. His achievements are all the more impressive when you consider how much catching up he had to do. In America, future athletic stars usually start young. Some NBA players were practically babies when they first got their hands on a basketball. Most went to schools with strong basketball programs and were well trained in the fundamentals by the time they reached college. Not so Rony, who grew up in the Middle East. He had raw talent but little experience when he first showed up on the Syracuse campus.

That was in the summer of 1982. Coach Jim Boeheim was in his office worrying about where he'd find a really tall basketball player. SU is a power in college basketball, but every basketball power goes after the seven-footers with gusto. Suddenly, a towering figure loomed in the doorway. The towering figure was Rony Seikaly, eager to play for Syracuse. The Orange had located its big man.

How did a teenager living in Greece happen upon SU? Actually, Rony was no stranger to Syracuse. His family has deep roots in the city. His father was even born there. Rony's sister attended SU, and his brother went to nearby Colgate. It was his brother who first took Rony to see a basketball game at SU. The dome was electric with excitement, and as he listened to the roar of the crowd he decided then and there to become an Orangeman. It would be tough making the transition from Greece to America, but since Rony had so many relatives in Syracuse, the snowy upstate city felt friendly and warm. It was like a second home.

Home is a charged word for Rony. Although he is an American citizen, home for Rony and his parents is Lebanon. Rony's grandparents were merely visiting America when Rony's father was born.

Torn apart by warring factions, Lebanon is a hotbed of violence and terrorism. Spending the first ten years of his life in Lebanon has left Rony with more than his share of painful memories. His family moved to Greece so that their children could grow up safely. Rony attended the American School in Athens. It was there that the future SU center first played basketball.

Playing basketball in Athens isn't like playing

Rony Seikaly. *(Courtesy Syracuse University)*

basketball in the United States, which is the basketball headquarters of the world. Rony never played in an officiated game, and all the centers he faced were under six feet tall. Luckily, Rony got some help from a Greek professional team playing in Athens. He wasn't allowed to join the team because he wasn't a Greek citizen, but at least he was allowed to practice with the players.

That adds up to woefully limited training for someone about to play basketball on a Big East Conference team in America. Understandably, Rony had to struggle to learn the basics and keep up with more advanced players. In the beginning, his offense lagged behind his defensive development, and he sometimes lost his concentration. But striving for all he was worth paid off for Rony Seikaly, who's now one of the most outstanding athletes in college basketball. A plus for Rony was his ability to take criticism and learn from his mistakes. Unlike a number of gifted athletes, Rony Seikaly does not have an ego problem.

Rony knows what it's like to come back from an injury, too. During tryouts for the 1986 gold medal–winning U.S. World Games team, Rony suffered a stress fracture in his left foot. He made the team, played through the pain, but had to wear a cast on his foot after the games ended. It was a scary time. Not only did Rony miss valuable preseason training, but he also had to worry about his future. Stress fractures can be serious. Fortunately, all was well, and Rony burst onto the 1986–87 sports scene ready for action.

What is the wealthy, good-looking, talented Rony Seikaly like off-court? Not surprisingly, his closest friends are students from other countries, chiefly the Middle East. Ask them what Rony's like, and they'll tell you he's a nice guy. And that's how most people who meet him describe Rony.

But Rony is more than nice. He's a quiet, sensitive person. After all, being six-foot-ten tends to set you apart from others. So does being uprooted from your country. No, he is definitely not your ordinary college athlete, and with all his talent you can expect Rony Seikaly to be someone quite out of the ordinary in the NBA, too.

If you'd like to get in touch with Rony Seikaly, write:

Sports Information Office
Syracuse University
Manley Field House
Syracuse, New York 13210

8

BORIS BECKER

They call West Germany's sports superstar several nicknames, including "Boom Boom" and the "Red Bomber." Whatever the nickname, there's never been anybody in tennis quite like Boris Becker, the six-foot-two red-haired champion who weighs a strong hundred and seventy-five pounds.

To be the tops in tennis, an athlete must win on the legendary fast grass courts of the All England Lawn Tennis and Croquet Club in Wimbledon. Björn Borg won Wimbledon when he was twenty. John McEnroe won when he was twenty-two. Jimmy Connors's turn came when he was twenty one. How old was Boris Becker when he won the men's singles title at Wimbledon? He was all of seventeen. That makes him the youngest winner in history.

That was in 1985. Boris went on to survive a tough tournament schedule and a blaze of publicity to win Wimbledon again in 1986. Since then, Boris's career has had its ups and downs, but he has remained one of the leading tennis players in the world. He's certainly one of the most famous.

Boris started playing tennis when he was only three years old. His father, Karl-Heinz Becker, was an architect who counted tennis as one of his favorite hobbies. He even designed the very tennis court where baby Boris began swinging a racket.

Boris was born on November 22, 1967, in Leimen, West Germany. Leimen is near Heidelberg, a city known for its university which is the oldest in Germany. As a child, Boris liked to play soccer as well as tennis. After all, soccer is the most popular sport in Europe. But the instructors at the Leimen tennis club spotted Boris's talent for tennis and saw to it that he received good, solid early training.

In Germany, junior tournaments are organized through the West German Tennis Federation, and by the age of nine Boris was competing regularly and winning regularly. Even in those days, he was known as a stubborn, tough, and aggressive tennis player. He was so aggressive and competitive that the Federation suspended him briefly from their youth program. The freckle-faced kid may have looked angelic, but he wasn't.

But suspensions were a thing of the past when at age twelve Boris decided to devote himself solely to tennis. He said goodbye to soccer and worked out daily with his trainer, Gunther Bosch. Bosch was molding Boris into a champion. In 1982, Boris won West Germany's junior championship. His first big international competition came in 1983, when he was runner-up in the U.S. junior championship.

Then came one of those moments that change people's lives. Boris met Ion Tiriac, who had coached tennis greats Ilie Nastase and Björn Borg. Tiriac didn't want to be Boris's coach. He wanted to become Boris's manager and promote his career. But that meant Boris would have to give up his amateur status. Was he too young for such a big step? Would he be good enough to compete at the professional level? Tiriac believed Boris had the ability and the drive, and after thinking things over Boris and his parents agreed.

Tiriac turned out to be a very clever manager. The brooding Romanian ex-coach and ex-player who says he is descended from the fourteenth-century nobleman who served as the model for the Count Dracula of fiction made Boris work hard from the start. No sooner did Boris graduate from high school than Tiriac sent him off on a grueling round of tournaments. He also made sure that Boris practiced daily and did a lot of exercises.

Boris proved he was championship material by doing everything he was asked to do, and then some. Even injuring his ankle and taking time out for surgery couldn't stop him for long. For one full year, he worked on perfecting his booming, powerful serve. By the time Wimbledon rolled around, Boris had scored some important wins. He was unseeded at Wimbledon, and nobody expected him to win. What followed was one wonderful Wimbledon. A stunned crowd watched Boris beat his opponents and reach the final encounter.

Enter Kevin Curran, who was ten years older than Boris Becker. That meant a full extra decade of training and experience. When Curran faced Boris across the net in the final match, he had just defeated some of tennis's top names. Beating Boris should have been a cinch. But it wasn't. Boris outhit Curran, outguessed him, outlasted him, and outshone him. When the dust settled at Wimbledon, there emerged a new world champion. Boom Boom Boris had arrived.

In a way, what happened after Boris's Wimbledon win is even more astonishing than the win itself. Boris shot to a level of superstardom in his native West Germany which can hardly be imagined in America. It would take a history lesson to fully explain why this occurred. But the Nazi era in Germany and Germany's loss of World War II are at the heart of it.

Boris Becker. *(Chase Roe/Retna Ltd.)*

Boris explained things this way to *Time* magazine: "The Germans were waiting for somebody. They were searching for another hero. The Americans could say they were Americans and be proud. But the Germans never liked to say they were Germans outside their own country. Now it often happens that they say 'We are Germans—from the land of Boris Becker.' That's my achievement."

West Germany fell so wildly in love with the appealing fresh-faced teenager that the country was gripped by a national frenzy. A poll revealed that the only name better known in Germany than Boris Becker was Volkswagen. Boris's hometown greeted his return from Wimbledon with a celebration that dwarfed anything this side of a ticker-tape parade in New York.

Fan mail poured in. Magazines and newspapers featured front-page pictures of Boris and stories about him every day. Politicians wanted to have their pictures taken with Boris. One of Boris's inexpensive tennis rackets was auctioned off for thousands of dollars. Girls sent him love letters. Fans followed him around the streets and around the world. He was named sports ambassador of UNICEF.

Boris's father and his mother, Elvira, did their best to shield him from the uproar, but it was impossible. To get away from many of the reporters who pursued him, Boris signed an exclusive contract with one of West Germany's major newspapers. Meanwhile, Ion Tiriac saw to it that Boris Becker, "hot property," earned plenty of money.

Boris signed an estimated twenty-four-million-dollar contract with the West German sporting goods firm Puma. Financially juicy arrangements were worked out for him with a Dutch electronics conglomerate, a German watch manufacturer, and a bank. Boris's yearly earnings from product endorsements and prize money won on the pro tennis circuit may run as high as from four and a half million dollars to an even more staggering ten million.

Despite the glory of being a world-champion tennis player and the heady excitement of the lucrative promotional deals, there is a down side to Boris Becker's success story. Picture yourself being so famous you couldn't leave your house without being mobbed by fans. Okay, at first it would be flattering. But as time wore on, you might grow tired of all the attention. You'd never have any privacy. You couldn't even walk around the corner to buy a soda without people bothering you. You wouldn't be able to go to a restaurant or a movie or a game with your friends without being hounded. People you had never met before would follow you around and beg you for your autograph or try to take your picture.

Boris Becker isn't a movie star or a rock star. Models and movie stars sometimes thrive on that kind of public attention. Boris is an athlete who spends most of his time playing tennis. He doesn't enjoy the worshipping fans, and he'd just as soon the photographers and interviewers left him alone. For one thing, it's tough to play tennis in the blazing glare of so much publicity. For another thing, it's tough to live up to being a national hero.

Being human, Boris isn't always able to ignore the publicity and behave coolly on the court. He has been known to break his tennis racket and throw tennis balls when he's on the losing side of the net. After several spats and rows, Boris and trainer Gunther Bosch have gone their separate ways. When Boris decided to leave Germany and move to Monte Carlo, many Germans became angry, accusing him of leaving Germany to avoid paying taxes.

Boris claims he moved to Monte Carlo to find some privacy. People leave him alone there, and he's free to come and go as he pleases. When he's not playing tennis, Boris spends his time listening to rock music and going to movies with his latest girlfriend, Benedicte Courtin, a law student. No wild spender, Boris's only big expense recently was a shiny sports car.

A likable, basically ordinary person, Boris Becker isn't trying to be a charismatic superstar. Others have thrust that role upon him. He just wants to be what he already is, a super tennis player whose name will go down in the record books. The Wimbledon wins of 1985 and 1986 mean the name Boris Becker is already in the record books, etched in gold. Future wins will make the name gleam even brighter.

———————

To get in touch with Boris Becker, or to find out more about professional tennis, write:

Association of Tennis Professionals
611 Ryan Plaza Drive
Arlington, Texas 76011

You can also write:

Boris Becker
c/o Deutscher Sportbund
Otto Fleck Schneise 12-D
6000 Frankfurt-am-Main
71 West Germany

9

SPUD WEBB

His name is Anthony Jerome Webb, but everybody calls him by his nickname, "Spud." He's basketball's Mighty Mite, the smallest guy ever to play regularly in the NBA. Making it to the NBA is an oversized dream for somebody who's five-foot seven. Not surprisingly, a lot of people told Spud he didn't have a chance. But he kept right on working hard, dreaming big, and reaching for the stars. He got his wish, and today the hundred-and-thirty-three-pound Spud is a first-rate athlete who has justly earned his place on the roster of the NBA's Atlanta Hawks.

The speedy Spud can do a lot with a basketball. Watch his quickness when he's dribbling a ball on the open floor. He can shoot from the outside, and he can penetrate just about any defense and make it look easy.

But he's at his spectacular best when it comes to the dunk. Then it seems he has rockets in his shoes. Spud's vertical leap is an amazing forty-two inches. He won the 1986 NBA slam dunk title on February 9, 1986, in Dallas. Many experts predicted he'd win the title again in 1987, but an injury kept him from competing.

As a backup point guard, Spud knows how to block shots and has even been called for goaltending. His ability to stand tall in midair has won him the respect of the giants who people the NBA. Remember, many of the men in the NBA are six-foot-seven or taller. Being so very short by pro basketball standards has forced Spud to use his brains. He's very clever at coming up with the creative play and the surprising steal.

You may think Spud got his short, catchy nickname because of his size, but he didn't. *Spud* is also another word for *potato,* but that has nothing to do with his name either. Spud's odd nickname came to him in a funny way. He was born in Dallas, Texas, on July 13, 1963, a few years after the Russians had launched a round artificial satellite into space named *Sputnik.* A friend of the Webbs visiting the hospital to see newborn baby Anthony Jerome joked that the baby's head looked like *Sputnik.* The name stuck, and along the way *Sputnik* got shortened to *Sput* and wound up *Spud.*

Spud's parents run the Webb Soul Market, a

Spud Webb. *(Courtesy Atlanta Hawks)*

food store near the Cotton Bowl in Dallas. Spud, the second of five children, went to Wilmer-Hutchins High School in Dallas. Then he attended Midland Junior College, where he played basketball with dazzling skill. He led Midland to the 1982 National Junior College (JUCO) title as well as a 65-and-8 record in two seasons. He was named first-team all-JUCO as a sophomore and was a two-time all-conference and all-regional selection at Midland.

Thanks to this outstanding record, Spud was recruited by North Carolina State. But Coach Jim Valvano was doubtful. Spud's size seemed a real handicap, although he quickly proved that he was a terrific athlete who also had a lot of faith in himself. Soon Coach Valvano had a lot of faith in Spud. Spud started forty-nine of sixty-six games for the Wolfpack. He holds a one-game assist record with eighteen versus Northeastern in 1984. In the two seasons he was there, Spud led North Carolina State in assists, leaving school in fourth place on the all-time assist list.

So far so good, but even at its best college basketball is not the NBA. How would Spud fare when it came to the big time? After being drafted by the Detroit Pistons in 1985, he found his real home with a team that favors the fast break, the Atlanta Hawks. The Hawks' head coach, Mike Fratello, could understand a five-foot-seven player because Fratello's five-foot-seven himself.

Spud's rookie season set to rest the rumors that he couldn't keep up with the towering tall men of the NBA. He set a Hawk playoff record with eighteen assists versus Detroit on April 19, scored in double figures in twenty-five games with three games of twenty-plus points, and had nine games with ten-plus assists in regular season. He continued playing well the following season, though injuries were a problem.

For someone as small as Spud, the possibility of receiving a serious injury in NBA play is very real. That makes his boldness and courage on the court even more impressive. It's one thing to play boldly when you're seven feet tall. Who's going to intimidate you? When you're Spud's size and you refuse to be intimidated, that's really something.

Not surprisingly, Spud Webb's talent coupled with his size have made him a phenomenon in the sport of basketball. He brings the fans in to home games. After he won the 1986 NBA slam dunk contest, he became popular with the many fans across the country who had watched him win on TV. Commercials and endorsements followed. The Hawks sometimes play up Spud's size. For example, they had a Spud Webb "sticker night," which would have been a "poster night" if Spud had been taller.

But the Hawks have been careful not to treat Spud like a toy. In the world of basketball, he is seen as a genuinely fine athlete who has succeeded despite his height and weight. Silly promotional campaigns that made too much of his size have been vetoed.

To begin with, five-foot-seven isn't short outside of basketball. Lots of men are that height. Even in the annals of basketball, there have been two other players as short as Spud—Wat Misaka and Red Klotz. Both, however, weighed a solid twenty pounds more than Spud. Both also played decades ago, when basketball players in general tended to be shorter. Neither played as long as Spud has or was as spectacular on the court. Five-foot-three (or less) Tyrone "Muggsy" Bogues of Wake Forest was a high draft choice for the NBA this season. How he will do in pro basketball is as yet unknown.

Off the court, Spud is a pleasant, quiet person who lives in Marietta, an Atlanta suburb. When he's not thinking about basketball, he's thinking about football. Spud is a fanatic Dallas Cowboys fan and a close friend of Cowboys' defensive back, Dexter Clinckscale.

Can Spud Webb continue to thrive in the land of giants? He does worry about his future and the constant pressure he's under to prove himself. But so far, Anthony Jerome "Spud" Webb's motto has been "Giants beware."

Spud Webb

To get in touch with Spud Webb, write:

Atlanta Hawks
100 Techwood Drive, N.W.
Atlanta, Georgia 30303

10

KRISTIE PHILLIPS

She's only four-foot-ten, which means she's got to look up when she's talking to someone even five feet tall. She only weighs eighty pounds. But her size is just right for gymnastics, and at age fifteen Kristie Phillips is already a leader in her sport. Besides having gobs of talent, Kristie has other assets, including a perky personality, a cute face topped by a mop of reddish-blond hair, and a bright silvery smile—silvery because she's got a mouth full of braces like a lot of other teenagers.

At age thirteen, Kristie was the youngest American ever to enter the prestigious McDonald's American Cup. She won it, defeating gymnasts from nineteen other countries. Since then, she's added win after win in national and international competition. That means she's got quite a collection of gold medals. Her dream—the dream of all gymnasts—is to win an Olympic gold medal someday, the shiniest gold of all.

If you're familiar with gymnastics, you know there are four womens' events: vault, uneven parallel bars, balance beam, and floor exercise. Though Kristie loves the floor exercise and is a fine vaulter, she's at her best on the beam. Her grace, strength, and flexibility are amazing. On the beam she can turn herself into a human donut, then stretch her legs and do a split. The official name of this move is a straddle reverse planche, and it's Kristie's specialty. It's really special when you realize the balance beam is only four inches wide.

Though Kristie was born in Baton Rouge, Louisiana, she makes her home in Houston, Texas, these days. That's because Houston is where you'll find coach Bela Karolyi, who trained the greatest female gymnast ever, Nadia Comaneci, superstar of the seventies. Karolyi still lived in his native Romania then. He defected to the United States in 1981 and began molding champion American gymnasts, including the 1984 Olympic gold medal winner, Mary Lou Retton.

The choice of a coach is very important to a gymnast. It's not just a question of physical training. A good coach must have the right rapport with a gymnast, must help the gymnast feel confident. Karolyi likes and understands his students. You can tell by watching him work with Kristie.

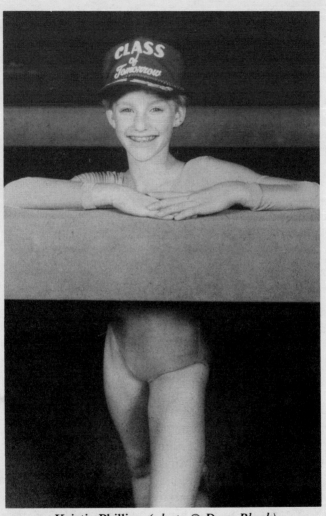

Kristie Phillips. *(photo © Dave Black)*

Whenever she wins a major competition, she runs straight to Karolyi, who gives her a proud hug.

It was during the 1976 Olympics that Kristie Phillips, only four, switched on a television set and got her first glimpse of Nadia Comaneci. It was her first view of gymnastics. Despite being little more than a tot, Kristie was already a poised and charming performer. She was the youngest in a family of four children and the only girl. Kristie's family entered her in a beauty contest when she was one year old. Before she was two, she was taking modeling lessons. Dancing lessons followed, and by the age of four Kristie was already an old pro when it came to pleasing judges and winning applause from audiences. But the sight of Nadia on television made Kristie forget about modeling and dancing. From now on it would be gymnastics.

Kristie began her training in Baton Rouge, never dreaming that her hero, Nadia's coach, would one day coach her. At that point, Kristie and Bela Karolyi seemed to be on two opposite and even rival paths. After all, Karolyi was from faroff Transylvania, the same Transylvania made famous in America by another Bela, Bela Lugosi of the Count Dracula movies.

Karolyi didn't start out as a gymnast. An all-around talented athlete, he represented his country in the 1956 Olympics as a hammer thrower. Next he turned to handball, a popular sport in

Romania. In 1959, after playing on the Romanian handball team, Karolyi won a scholarship to the University of Bucharest. In college, he had so much trouble with the gymnastics classes that he almost flunked out of school. Then he met his wife-to-be, Marta, a gifted gymnast. With her help, he grew so skillful that he made the college gymnastics team. He went on to receive a degree in physical education, and he and Marta teamed up to teach children their favorite sport. They began their work in a coal-mining town in the Carpathian Mountains of Transylvania.

The couple had a lot of new ideas. One was to start kids in gymnastics very young. Some people accused the Karolyis of starting kids too young. At that time, gymnastics champions were usually in their middle to late twenties. But the Karolyis didn't believe gymnastics training was in any way harmful to children. They felt then, and still feel, that working hard at gymnastics from an early age makes one strong and healthy.

The world soon learned that the Karolyis knew how to produce winners. In 1967, the duo's well-coached team won Romania's national championships. In 1975, their team took the European championships, with Nadia Comaneci winning no less than five gold medals. The Karolyis continued to perfect their training program in Houston. What they look for besides body type and raw talent is the athlete with competitive spirit. And competitive spirit is just what Kristie Phillips has.

Of course, it took time for Kristie and Karolyi to find each other. After training in hometown Baton Rouge, Kristie spent two useful years with coach Vannie Edwards in Shreveport, Louisiana. The move to Shreveport put a lot of pressure on the Phillips family and shows just how devoted Kristie's parents are when it comes to their daughter's gymnastics career. Although gymnastics may look very glamorous on television, in reality it takes a lot of hard work and even sacrifice on the part of everyone involved, and that includes the parents and brothers and sisters of gymnasts as well as the gymnasts themselves.

When Kristie went to Shreveport with her mother, her father had to stay in Baton Rouge working and keeping an eye on his three sons. It wasn't easy, but the family was determined to give the talented Kristie every chance to develop into a first-rate athlete. Kristie's mother, Terri, had been quite an athlete herself in high school. She was left halfback on a girl's football team in Wisner, Louisiana. Terri was a tough player, and she was also tough enough to handle the loneliness of leaving her husband and sons while caring for Kristie. In Shreveport, Terri worked as a house-mother, minding a group of Vannie Edwards's gymnastics students.

The next move for Kristie was to Atlanta, where

her mother earned money by taking care of the new coach's children and cooking for the coach's family. By working for and with Kristie's various coaches, Terri was able to be near her daughter at all times. She didn't want a job that kept her away from her daughter, because young athletes uprooted from their homes need emotional as well as financial support. Not surprisingly, Terri and Kristie are very close, and Kristie knows that her mother is there whenever she needs her.

As for the financial side of creating a top gymnast, it might surprise you to learn that it costs a hefty twenty thousand dollars or so a year. In Houston, Terri rents a house and is housemother for several young gymnasts. She even boards dogs to pick up extra money. It's been Houston for Terri since 1982, because that's when Kristie took a major leap forward, tumbling right into Bela and Marta Karolyi's little group of American gymnastic super-talents. Kristie was with Nadia's coach at last.

What is life like for an aspiring teenage gymnast? Like most teenagers, Kristie goes to school, Westfield High in Houston. When she's not studying or hard at work in the gym or en route to a competition, she likes to go swimming or water skiing. As far as friends go, there are the other gymnasts.

Kristie isn't the only dazzling talent in gymnastics or the only student the Karolyis coach,

Kristie Phillips. *(photo © Dave Black)*

Kristie Phillips and coach Bela Karolyi. *(photo © Dave Black)*

and, though rival gymnasts have to compete against each other, they're still close friends. They spend a lot of time together, and they all care about the same thing—their sport. That sets them apart from other teenagers and brings them together.

Besides Kristie, three gymnasts the Karolyis have a lot to be proud of are Phoebe Mills, Julissa D'Anne Gomez, and Robin Lynn Carter. Like Kristie, they are coached by the Karolyis and have the drive, energy, talent, and potential it takes to reach for the gold.

Phoebe, age fifteen, is a former speed skating champion who comes from Northfield, Illinois. Her five brothers and sisters are all competitive skaters, but for Phoebe it's all gymnastics now, though she still skates as a hobby.

Julissa, also fifteen, comes from San Antonio, Texas, and goes to the same high school as Kristie. Her first love was ballet, but at age five she switched to gymnastics. Athletic accomplishments tell only part of the story of Julissa. She reads a lot, likes doing crossword puzzles, and wants to become an astronomy professor someday.

Robin Lynn is the youngest of the trio, born on January 27, 1973, in Denver, Colorado. Outside of gymnastics, she's interested in art.

Even though girls get the lion's share of attention in gymnastics, there are plenty of boys involved in the sport. By and large, male gymnasts reach their peak at a later age than female gymnasts partly because the sport requires enormous upper body and arm strength in males. Men's events feature floor exercise, pommel horse, still rings, vault, parallel bars, and horizontal bars. One rising star among the boys is Emilio Marrero, who's eighteen and lives in New York, where he is coached by Roberto Pumpido. Emilio lives with his mother, a waitress, in East Harlem. He loves working out on the rings, and in his free time he likes to watch movies with dazzling special effects. His favorite hobby is sort of unusual—snakes.

So keep your eye on Phoebe, Julissa, Robin, and Emilio. But most of all, keep watching Kristie Phillips, gymnastics' senational new superstar. She may be small, but she's one big competitor.

To get in touch with Kristie Phillips, or to find out more about gymnastics, write:

U.S. Gymnastics Federation
Marketing and Communications Department
1099 North Meridian, Suite 380
Indianapolis, Indiana 46204

11

DAVID RIVERS

It all happened very suddenly on an August morning in 1981. The van was coming down County Road 1 in rural Indiana. At the intersection with County Road 30, a car pulled out unexpectedly. The driver of the van hit the brakes. The braking car skidded on the gravel at the side of the road and went out of control. It flew into the air, rolled over, and crashed into a ditch.

Miraculously, the driver received only a minor gash on the leg. But, as so often happens in accidents like this, the passenger was not so lucky. He was thrown through the windshield. The broken, jagged glass left a gash more than a foot long in his abdomen. He lay there on the ground bleeding heavily.

The young man who had been driving the van was Ken Barlow, a member of the Notre Dame

David Rivers. *(Courtesy University of Notre Dame, photo by Steven Navratil)*

basketball team. His passenger was David Rivers, Notre Dame's classy and exciting point guard and the number one player on the team.

Let's stop here for a minute. With all the bad publicity college athletes have been getting, we have to make a point. Tests showed that neither man had any drugs or alcohol in his system. They weren't speeding or doing anything dangerous. They were just driving to the home of a local caterer who often hired Notre Dame basketball players so that they could earn some extra money in the summer. What happened on the road that morning was an accident—pure and simple and terrible.

As a result of that accident, David Rivers was horribly injured, and he was sure he was going to die. Rivers's death would have been a double tragedy. Not only would the life of an extremely talented young athlete be cut short, but he was a young man who had already ovecome so much.

The van had landed in the tall grass, and David was thrown a distance from the wreck. At first Barlow couldn't find him. When he did, he asked Rivers if he was all right.

"No, I'm not all right," said David.

Then Barlow saw all the blood. "David, don't die," he pleaded.

There was a house nearby, and Barlow used the phone to call the hospital. An ambulance arrived quickly. Rivers was conscious throughout the ordeal. He recalls being remarkably calm. He says that he felt "disappointed" and a little "alarmed." But he didn't really panic.

If you can call anyone who has just been in a serious accident lucky, David Rivers was lucky. Though the cut was severe and deep, no important organs had been injured. After a three-hour operation, it was clear to the doctors that David would live. The next question was, would he ever be able to play basketball again, and if so, how soon?

Most doctors figured that, barring complications, Rivers would certainly be able to work his basketball magic again. However, they doubted he could play during the 1986–87 season, which was only a few months away. They didn't count on David's determination. By the third week in September, he was not only out of bed, he was riding a bike fifteen minutes a day. The next week he was swimming, and a short time later he was jogging. He started practicing basketball in the swimming pool. By early December, David was back as the starting point guard for Notre Dame.

Overall, the Notre Dame season was good but not spectacular. David Rivers's season was spectacular, even though he still wasn't back to one hundred percent of his previous physical ability.

David Rivers was born in a housing project in Jersey City, New Jersey. He was one of fourteen children. His father worked two jobs, and his mother was a hotel maid. Sometimes there still wasn't enough money to go around.

The Jersey City project was a tough place to grow up. One of David's brothers was stabbed to death. Another was run over by a truck. Yet, despite all the hardship and the tragedy, David Rivers became, and has remained, a remarkably optimistic person.

Like many kids in the projects, David spent a lot of time on the playground basketball courts. He wasn't particularly large, so he developed other skills. He was very fast and could dribble behind his back and between his legs. The bigger men couldn't catch him. Most of all, he knew how to see everything that was going on around him. He could anticipate what other players were going to do.

A lot of basketball players, particularly young ones, have only one idea: get the ball, get to the basket, and shoot. David was too small to get over the big men. But he always seemed to know when someone else on his team was open, and he could pass the ball there. The opposing team could never figure out what he was doing. He would drive one way, look another, and pass the ball off in a third direction. Fouling him wasn't any use, because he developed into a great free-throw shooter. More than that, he could pass the ball not to where his teammate was but to where he was going to be. That's called great anticipation. Pretty soon, everybody in the playground wanted to have "little" David Rivers on their team.

His basketball skills earned David a scholarship to Notre Dame, long known as one of the leading sports schools in the country. But unlike some schools, Notre Dame is very serious about student athletes really being students. Athletes have to keep their grades up. David admits that the classroom work at Notre Dame has been tough for him. He needs a C average, and he's been making it, but with little to spare.

If he's no whiz in the classroom, on the court he's pure magic. He's one of the most intelligent players in the college game today. Notre Dame basketball coach Digger Phelps says, "He knows what the nine other people are doing on the court like no one I've ever seen. The game of basketball belongs to him."

Though he's only six feet tall and weighs one hundred eighty pounds—small for a professional basketball player, small even for a big-time college basketball player—David certainly plans a professional career. The NBA scouts are already beaming in anticipation. But there is one more goal between David and the NBA. He should be eligible for the 1988 Olympic basketball team. With David Rivers playing point guard for the United States, the rest of the world had better watch out.

David Rivers

To get in touch with David Rivers, write:

*Sports Information Department
University of Notre Dame
Notre Dame, Indiana 46536*

12

WOMEN IN SPORTS

When we prepared the list of young sports superstars for this book, we realized that it was unbalanced. There are nine men and only two women. We could have included a few other well-known young women athletes. But we also could have included a lot more well-known men.

The simple truth is that there just *are* a lot more well-known male athletes. Women do become famous in certain sports, like gymnastics and figure skating. In these sports, women often become more famous than men, and we have a couple of examples in this book. Women can also become well known in some other sports—tennis and golf, for example.

In 1988, you're going to hear a lot about women athletes, because 1988 is an Olympic year. In the Olympics, women compete on an equal, or nearly

Ellen Mullarkey, University of Iowa volleyball.
(Courtesy University of Iowa)

equal, footing with men. Often, women Olympians are the big stars of the games. Think about some of the famous Olympians of past years—Dorothy Hamill, Peggy Fleming, Nadia Comaneci, and Mary Lou Retton.

The status of women athletes in the United States has been improving over the years. At one time a lot of people thought women were not even physically capable of running a marathon. Now the best women marathoners are posting times that would have been record performances for men not too many years ago. Women are also beginning to excel in other sports once thought to be exclusively male, including power lifting and even arm wrestling.

But there are still some big gaps, and the biggest is in team sports. There is not a single major professional women's team in any sport in America. Okay, so women don't play football. They don't play baseball either, though they surely could. It's always softball, which can be an exciting and demanding game when played by people who really know what they are doing.

But what about basketball? Women's basketball is played under rules not very different from those of men's basketball. In a few colleges, women's basketball is treated as a major sport. But have you ever attended a women's college basketball game? Have you ever seen one on television? Major tournament games are televised, but rarely

Page Dunlap, standout member of the Lady Gators golf team. *(Courtesy University of Florida, photo by Tim Black)*

Shaun Stafford, Lady Gators tennis. *(Courtesy University of Florida)*

by the networks and never in prime time. Even here there are signs of change. With the growth of cable television and cable TV networks devoted exclusively to sports, women's basketball is getting much more attention and seems to be drawing larger audiences. Perhaps someday terrific players like Andrea Lloyd of the University of Texas or Tonya Edwards of the University of Tennessee will get the kind of recognition they deserve.

How about volleyball? Granted, it's not considered a major sport for men or women in America. But don't think a volleyball game played by an Olympic-class team is the same game you may have played at the beach—it isn't. It's a tough and demanding game to play and an exciting one to watch. In some colleges, women's volleyball is a major sport. There have also been attempts to create professional women's volleyball.

So things are getting better, although there is still a long way to go. In most high schools and colleges, the female athletes don't get the sort of programs or encouragement they need. However, if you're a sports-minded girl, there are quite a number of colleges and universities in the country that have truly first-rate women's athletic departments. We have listed four of the best-known schools below, but there are others. Go for it, girls!

Kamie Ethridge, former star, now student coach of the Lady Longhorns, University of Texas women's basketball team. *(Courtesy University of Texas)*

University of Tennessee
Women's Athletic Department
115 Stokely Athletic Center
Knoxville, Tennessee 37919

University of Iowa
Iowa City, Iowa 52242

University of Texas
Women's Sports Information
606 Bellmont
Austin, Texas 78712

University of Florida
P.O. Box 14485
Gainsville, Florida 32604

ABOUT THE AUTHORS

DANIEL COHEN is the author of more than a hundred books for young readers and adults. SUSAN COHEN is the author of several gothic novels and mysteries. The Cohens have coauthored a wide range of books for children and teenagers including *Heroes of the Challenger; Rock Video Superstars; Rock Video Superstars II; Wrestling Superstars; Wrestling Superstars II;* and *Young and Famous: Hollywood's Newest Superstars,* all of which are available in Archway Paperback editions.

Daniel Cohen is a former managing editor of *Science Digest* magazine and has a degree in journalism from the University of Illinois. Susan Cohen holds a master's degree in social work from Adelphi University. Both grew up in Chicago where they married, later moving to New York.